BRINKLEY THE BAT

in

'Acrobat'

BY

T.N. CRAWFORD

AuthorHouse™ UK
1663 Liberty Drive
Bloomington, IN 47403 USA
www.authorhouse.co.uk
UK TFN: 0800 0148641 (Toll Free inside the UK)
UK Local: 02036 956322 (+44 20 3695 6322 from outside the UK)

This book is printed on acid-free paper.

ISBN: 979-8-8230-8773-5 (sc)
979-8-8230-8775-9 (hc)
979-8-8230-8774-2 (e)

Library of Congress Control Number: 2024910289

Print information available on the last page.

Published by AuthorHouse 05/22/2024

author

BRINKLEY THE BAT

in

'Acrobat'

Emerging from the dark, who is that?
a flying ace in his habitat,
warm in his velvet fur,
he's beginning to stir,
why it's Brinkley, the Pipistrelle bat!

On Summer nights, when the air is clear,
he flies through the trees, with little fear,
all around him he hears,
with magnificent ears,
the smallest bat, Brinkley's a dear!

The time to see Brinkley is by night,

and with hairless wings, he takes flight,

from out of a hollow,

he's too quick to follow,

doing this with hardly any sight!

When the sun goes down, and it gets dark,
he clambers out on to the tree bark,
with his sonar tuned in,
and a wide hungry grin,
Brinkley's flying over Primrose Park.

For Brinkley there's no need to go far,
with 'pings and clicks', he knows where they are,
as the moths flutter by,
catching them in the sky,
eating on the wing is nothing bizarre!

Starting with Brinkley, their numbers grew,
in a cauldron of bats, he flew,
there was a crying sound,
rising up from the ground,
Brinkley knew then what he had to do!

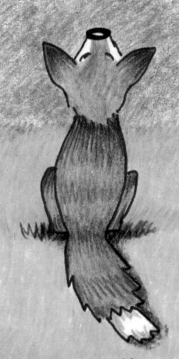

As the young cub's mum searched everywhere,

in a panic, she was in despair,

as her pup went astray,

wandering off to play,

the bats made an arrow in the air!

The young fox stayed calm,with all his might,
he had never had such a big fright,
and the bats really cared,
he was no longer scared,
the cub was found, much to their delight!

Mum and cub were together at last,

on silent wings,how the bats were fast,

so before the new day,

an aerial display,

with a final swoosh, the bats flew past!

Brinkley's breath turned colder, on the breeze,
he felt the start of Winter's freeze,
all huddled in their roost,
waiting for a warm boost,
from inside a hole, in the oak trees.

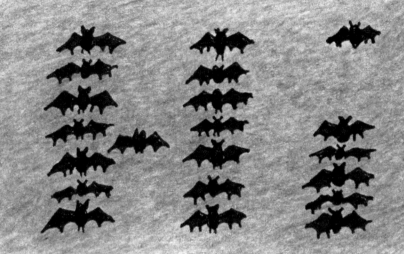

This ballet of bats, no longer seen,
a distant memory, where they'd been,
they will all hibernate,
'til the weather is great,
re-emerging, when everything's green!

Printed in the United States
by Baker & Taylor Publisher Services